FROM **TREE** TO **PAPER**

by Pam Marshall

Lerner Publications Company / Minneapolis

Lerner Publications Company
A division of Lerner Publishing Group
241 First Avenue North
Minneapolis, MN 55401 U.S.A.

Website address: www.lernerbooks.com

Library of Congress Cataloging-in-Publication Data

Marshall, Pam.
   From tree to paper / by Pam Marshall.
      p. cm. — (Start to finish)
   Includes index.
   Summary: Introduces the process through which trees are turned into paper.
   ISBN: 0–8225–0720–X (lib. bdg. : alk. paper)
   1. Paper—Juvenile literature. 2. Papermaking—Juvenile literature. [1. Paper. 2. Papermaking.] I. Title. II. Start to finish (Minneapolis, Minn.)
TS1105.5 .M37 2003
676—dc21   2001007206

Manufactured in the United States of America
2 3 4 5 6 – JR – 08 07 06 05 04 03

The photographs in this book appear courtesy of:
© W. Cody/Corbis, Cover; © Ron Sherman, pp. 1 (bottom), 19, 21; © Link/Visuals Unlimited, p. 1 (top); © Ellen B. Senisi/Photo Researchers, Inc, p. 3; © Inga Spence/Visuals Unlimited, p. 5; © Mark E. Gibson/Visuals Unlimited, p. 7; © David Lees/Corbis, pp. 9, 15; © Ned Therrien/Visuals Unlimited, p. 11; © Ed Kashi, p. 13; © Ecoscene/Corbis, p. 17; © Jim Whitmer/Visuals Unlimited, p. 23.

Table of Contents

We use paper every day.

How is it made?

Workers plant trees.

Most paper comes from trees.
Workers plant some trees just for
making paper. It takes many
years for a tree to get big.

Workers cut the trees.

Workers cut down tall, thick trees. They chop off the branches to make logs. Trucks take the logs to a **paper mill**. A paper mill is a place where paper is made.

A machine takes off bark.

A paper mill is full of machines. The first machine takes bark off the logs.

9

The logs are chopped.

A big machine called a **chipper** crushes and grinds the logs. The logs break apart into tiny chips of wood.

11

The wood is washed.

Other machines wash and smash the wood chips. **Pulp** pours out. Pulp is a wet, lumpy mix of ground-up wood and water.

Water drips down.

The wet pulp pours onto a screen. The screen lets the water drip down. Long, thin threads of wood called **fibers** stay on top. The wet fibers make a long piece of paper.

The paper is dried.

Heavy rollers squeeze more water out of the paper. Then hot rollers and ovens dry the paper.

The paper is rolled.

Machines wrap the dry paper onto huge rolls. The rolls are as tall as a grown-up person.

The paper is cut.

The paper is too big to be used. Workers feed it into machines that cut it. Some of the finished paper is sent to stores. Some is sent to factories for printing.

Read all about it!

Grab a newspaper, a comic book, or a magazine. All are made from paper, even this book!

Glossary

chipper (CHIP-ur): a machine that chops logs into wood chips

fibers (FYE-burz): long, thin threads of wood

paper mill (PAY-pur MILL): a place where paper is made

pulp (PUHLP): a mix of water and ground-up wood

Index